SEEKERS

KALLIK'S ADVENTURE

Seekers: Kallik's Adventure
Created by Erin Hunter
Written by Dan Jolley
Art by Bettina M. Kurkoski

Lettering - John Hunt
Production Artist - Lucas Rivera
Graphic Designer - Chelsea Windlinger

Editor - Lillian Diaz-Przybyl
Print Production Manager - Lucas Rivera
Managing Editor - Vy Nguyen
Senior Designer - Louis Csontos
Director of Sales and Manufacturing - Allyson De Simone
Associate Publisher - Marco F. Pavia
President and C.O.O. - John Parker
C.E.O. and Chief Creative Officer - Stu Levy

A **TOKYOPOP** Manga

TOKYOPOP and are trademarks or registered trademarks of TOKYOPOP Inc.

TOKYOPOP Inc.
5900 Wilshire Blvd. Suite 2000
Los Angeles, CA 90036

E-mail: info@TOKYOPOP.com
Come visit us online at www.TOKYOPOP.com

For information address HarperCollins Children's Books, a division of HarperCollins Publishers,
10 East 53rd Street, New York, NY 10022.
www.harpercollinschildrens.com

ISBN 978-0-06-172383-4
Library of Congress catalog card number: 2010939903

13 14 15 CG/BV 10 9 8 7 6 5 4 3
❖
First Edition

SEEKERS

KALLIK'S ADVENTURE

CREATED BY
ERIN HUNTER

WRITTEN BY
DAN JOLLEY

ART BY
BETTINA M. KURKOSKI

HAMBURG // LONDON // LOS ANGELES // TOKYO

HARPER
An Imprint of HarperCollinsPublishers

FOUR MONTHS LATER.

MAMA'S NOT GIVING US AS MUCH MILK AS SHE USED TO...

...AND WE HAVE TO POKE HER BELLY NOW TO GET ANY AT ALL.

A LOT OF THE TIME TAQQIQ GETS MORE MILK THAN I DO, 'CAUSE HE'S STRONGER.

THAT'S NOT FAIR AT ALL.

HEY! QUIT IT!

WELL, MOVE OVER, THEN! I'M HUNGRY, TOO!

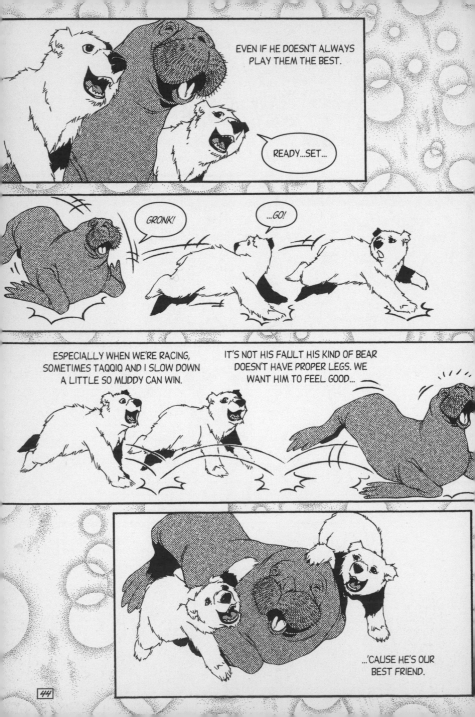

EVEN IF HE DOESN'T ALWAYS PLAY THEM THE BEST.

READY...SET...

GRONK!

...GO!

ESPECIALLY WHEN WE'RE RACING, SOMETIMES TAQQIQ AND I SLOW DOWN A LITTLE SO MUDDY CAN WIN.

IT'S NOT HIS FAULT HIS KIND OF BEAR DOESN'T HAVE PROPER LEGS. WE WANT HIM TO FEEL GOOD...

...'CAUSE HE'S OUR BEST FRIEND.

IT'S A SHAME WE CAN'T UNDERSTAND WHAT HE SAYS, BUT I DON'T THINK THAT MATTERS TOO MUCH.

WHENEVER WE GO DOWN TO THE ROCKS, HE'S EITHER RIGHT THERE WAITING FOR US...

...OR HE COMES AS SOON AS WE CALL FOR HIM.

MUDDY! MUUUUUDDY!

ARE YOU THERE?

PLAYING WITH MUDDY IS GREAT...

OH, MY PRECIOUS CUBS...

MY BEAUTIFUL LIGHTNING...MY HANDSOME LITTLE MOON...

I'M SO SORRY FOR LEAVING YOU! I NEVER THOUGHT A WALRUS WOULD COME ALL THE WAY TO THE DEN AND ATTACK YOU!

HOW DID IT EVER KNOW YOU WERE HERE?

I KNOW TAQQIQ AND I SHOULD TELL MAMA WHAT HAPPENED... BUT WE JUST CAN'T.

I THINK ABOUT THE WORD MAMA USED. "WALRUS?" IS THAT WHAT MUDDY IS?

IT'S SO CONFUSING. WAS THE BIG WALRUS ANGRY 'CAUSE WE'VE BEEN PLAYING WITH MUDDY? ...AND DID IT REALLY WANT TO EAT US?

MUDDY NEVER WANTED TO EAT US!

I CAN'T BELIEVE HOW MANY WALRUSES THERE ARE!

I TRY TO SPOT MUDDY AGAIN...AND FOR THE FIRST TIME, I CAN SEE PAST THE BIG ROCK RIDGE.

SURELY MUDDY'S OVER THERE SOMEWHERE.

BUT I CAN'T SEE HIM. I HOPE HE'S NOT TOO SAD WITHOUT TAQQIQ AND ME.

HE'S A WALRUS, AND WE'RE WHITE BEARS...I GUESS THAT MEANS WE CAN'T BE FRIENDS.

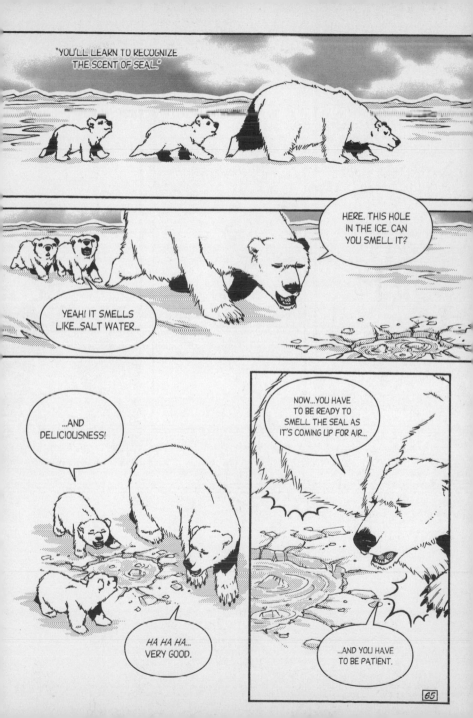

GLUB!

THE WATER'S SO COLD, IT FEELS LIKE IT'S FREEZING MY BRAIN, BUT...I CAN SEE SOMETHING...!

THOSE MUST BE SEALS! AND THEY'VE ALL SEEN ME!

OH, KALLIK, YOU CLUMSY, FOOLISH THING...YOU COULD HAVE DROWNED!

WELL, YOU'VE GONE AND DONE IT NOW

HAKK! HAKK!

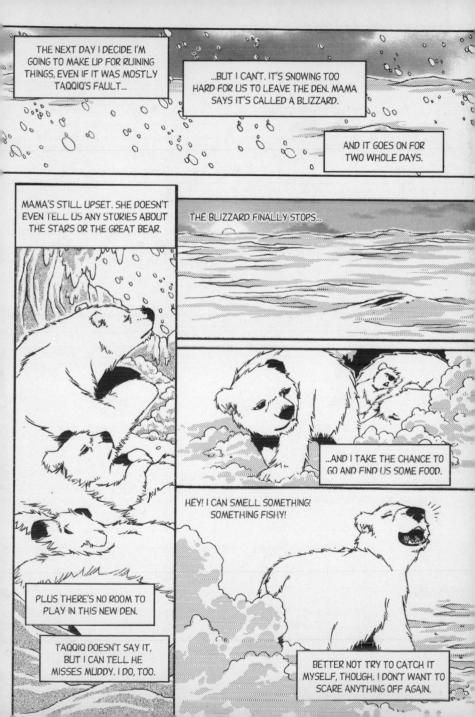

YEAH, BUT...WE'RE DANGEROUS TO THEM, TOO.

WHEN WE'RE BIGGER, YES.

I TRY TO SEE WHERE MUDDY'S GONE...SEE IF HE MADE IT BACK TO THE REST OF THE WALRUSES.

BUT I CAN'T EVEN TELL.

DON'T WORRY, PRECIOUS ONE.

BUT I WANT YOU TO KEEP ME SAFE, MAMA. I DON'T WANT TO HAVE TO SURVIVE ON MY OWN.

I PROMISE...YOU WON'T BE ON YOUR OWN FOR A LONG, LONG TIME.

UNTIL THEN, WE'LL ALL BE SAFE AND WELL FED ON THE ICE...

...ONCE YOU TWO LEARN HOW TO KEEP STILL WHEN YOU'RE WAITING FOR SEALS!

MAMA WILL KEEP US SAFE. I KNOW SHE WILL.

I JUST HOPE MUDDY STAYS SAFE, TOO.

GOOD-BYE, MUDDY!

...I'LL MISS YOU.

ERIN HUNTER

is inspired by a fascination with the ferocity of the natural world. As well as having great respect for nature in all its forms, Erin enjoys creating rich mythical explanations for animal behavior. She is also the author of the bestselling Warriors series.

Visit Erin Hunter online at www.warriorcats.com and www.seekerbears.com.

For exclusive information on your favorite authors and artists, visit www.authortracker.com.

DON'T MISS THE THIRD
SEEKERS MANGA:

SEEKERS

LUSA'S TALE

Black bear cub Lusa and her brother, Yogi, live in the Bear
Bowl, a curious place with fences on all sides. Every day, strange
flat-faces come to watch Lusa and her family over the edge of
the Bowl. This is the world that Lusa knows, but Lusa's father,
King, tells her stories of an outside world, one with no walls:
the wild. King tells her that no bear has ever left the Bowl, but
that doesn't stop Lusa from having some thrilling adventures
as she tries to learn about the world beyond!

TURN THE PAGE FOR A PEEK AT

SEEKERS

SPIRITS IN THE STARS

From the author of the #1 nationally bestselling Warriors series

SEEKERS

SPIRITS IN THE STARS

ERIN HUNTER

CHAPTER ONE

Ujurak

Ujurak's legs ached as he tried to concentrate on just putting one paw in front of another. He and his friends seemed to have been trudging across the Endless Ice forever, though he knew that only a few sunrises had passed since they'd escaped from the flat-faces near the oil rig.

Glancing over his shoulder, he could see that his three companions looked just as tired as he felt. Toklo, the big brown bear, shambled along with his head down. Lusa stumbled after him as if she hardly knew where she was anymore, her small shape a black dot against the endless white; Ujurak knew they would have to keep a close eye on her, for fear that she would sink back into the longsleep. Even Kallik, who was more at home on the ice than any of them, padded along with a grim expression.

All around them the ice had been carved and twisted by the wind into strange shapes, which sometime`s stretched over their heads into the sky. At first they had played hide-and-seek among them; Ujurak let out a small huff of amusement as he remembered how good Lusa was at hiding, in spite of her black pelt. Sometimes they would slide down the frozen drifts, or look for shapes that reminded them of animals. Toklo had growled at an ice pillar that he thought looked like Shoteka, the grizzly who had attacked him at Great Bear Lake.

But we're too tired for games now, Ujurak thought. *Too tired for anything except this endless slog.*

His heart sank further as he made out a frozen ridge across their path, a wall of ice that disappeared into the distance on either side.

"Now what?" Toklo grumbled, trudging up as Ujurak slowed to a halt. "Don't tell me we have to climb that."

"We do," Ujurak replied. He could feel that they were drawing closer and closer to the spirit of his mother, and the tugging on his paws was too strong to be ignored. "This is the way we must go."

Once the big grizzly would have argued with him. Now he just let out a snort of disgust. "I was afraid you were going to say that."

"But how?" Lusa asked, stifling a yawn. She and Kallik had plodded up next to them. "It's so high and smooth!"

Ujurak glanced at Kallik for advice, but the white bear only shook her head in confusion. "There were no ridges like this where I lived with Nisa and Taqqiq."

"I'll go first," Toklo announced. "I'll try to scrape some pawholds in the ice for the rest of you."

Without waiting for the others to respond, he began claw-
ing his way up the slippery slope. Ice splinters showered
down as he dug his claws into the surface; Lusa crouched and
wrapped her paws over her head. "Hey, that stings!" she protested.

"Come on, you'll be fine." Kallik nudged the small black
bear to her paws again. "You go next, and I'll give you a
boost."

Working her shoulders underneath Lusa, the white bear
heaved her upward. Lusa scrambled up the slope in Toklo's
wake, struggling to thrust her paws into the holes the bigger bear had made. She let out a startled yelp as she lost her
grip and began to slide down again, her forepaws splayed out
against the ice while her hindpaws scrabbled frantically. Ujurak let out a sigh of relief as he saw her drive her claws into a
gap in the surface and start climbing again.

"You next," Kallik suggested. "I'll keep watch for danger."

Ujurak agreed, though he wasn't sure they had much to
fear in this desolate landscape. He almost felt that they were
the only living creatures left in the world.

By now Toklo had reached the crest of the ridge and
turned to call back to his companions. "Come on! It's easier
on the other side!"

Ujurak climbed quickly, his paws strengthened by the
feeling that his mother was watching over them, and reached
the top of the ridge just behind Lusa.

The small black bear flopped down, panting. "I thought
we might be able to see land from up here," she said.

"But it's just more ice."

Gazing ahead, Ujurak saw that the ridge on this side sloped down gradually to an ice plain with a broken, choppy surface, like a frozen sea. The sky was covered with clouds, brightening to a milky radiance where the sun was trying to break through, and it was impossible to tell where the land ended and the sky began.

"We just have to keep going," Ujurak said.

As soon as Kallik arrived, shaking ice chips from her fur, they set off down the slope.

"I'm so tired my paws are falling off," Toklo grumbled, padding at Ujurak's side. "And my belly thinks my throat's been clawed out."

Ujurak pushed his snout into his friend's shoulder fur. "We'll stop to eat soon," he responded, trying to sound encouraging. "Kallik will hunt for us."

"She is good at that now," Toklo admitted. "Hey, Kallik, what about a nice fat seal?"

"Sure." Kallik raised her head, looking proud that Toklo was relying on her to provide for them. "Why don't you three rest, while I go and look for a seal hole?"

She paused, swinging her head around and sniffing— Ujurak guessed she was trying to sense the best place to start searching—then she plodded off across the ice.

Ujurak led the way to a twisted mass of snow that would give them some shelter against the wind that scoured the frozen plain. Lusa curled up in a hollow, wrapped one paw over her nose, and closed her eyes.

Toklo crouched beside her, scanning her anxiously. "I hope she's not falling into the longsleep," he muttered.

Ujurak nodded. Though Lusa had been more cheerful and active since they'd escaped from the flat-faces, he couldn't help worrying just as Toklo did. *She needs to reach land. We all do.*

The two brown bears huddled closer to Lusa, sharing their warmth, while they waited for Kallik.

"She'd better get a move on," Toklo remarked, shifting uneasily. "I'm starving!"

"Me too," Ujurak agreed.

"I'm sick of seal, though," the big grizzly went on. "What I wouldn't give for a fresh salmon, or a hare!"

Ujurak felt his mouth beginning to water, and his stomach rumbled at the thought. "I've heard Lusa muttering about grubs and berries in her dreams," he told his friend. "It won't be long now."

Toklo's only reply was a disbelieving grunt.

Ujurak couldn't help feeling optimistic. Awareness of his mother's presence tingled through him from his nose to his paws. But he didn't expect his companions to share his conviction. *They'll see,* he thought. *We must be near the end of our journey.*

Time dragged on, and Kallik did not return. Drowsily Ujurak let his mind drift back to the flat-face camp and to Sally, the young flat-face female who had been his friend. He remembered her dark hair and the laughter in her eyes, and the compassion she had shown when she was helping the animals who had been trapped in the oil. He remembered how shocked she had been when she'd seen him change back into a bear.

I wonder what she told the others about how Lusa and I disappeared? And will she try to find us again?

A pang of regret throbbed through Ujurak. It was weird to be missing a flat-face, and he knew it was best for them not to meet again. But he did miss Sally's cheerfulness and her kindness.

I'm not a flat-face; I'm a bear . . . aren't I? Not long ago he had almost lost the sense of who he really was when he had spent too long in whale shape. He didn't want to risk that, ever again. *I'm a bear. And how would I explain myself to Sally if we met again?*

"Uh . . . Sally, you see I'm mostly a bear, but sometimes I'm a flat-face, or a bird, or . . ." he muttered out loud.

"Hey!" Toklo prodded him in his side, bringing Ujurak fully awake again. "Are you talking to yourself?"

"No, I was talking to Sally," Ujurak replied, not thinking how this might sound to Toklo.

"What do you want to talk to her for?" There was a tinge of jealousy in Toklo's voice. "She's not even here. And she's a flat-face."

"She's a good flat-face," Ujurak protested. When Toklo huffed angrily, the smaller bear stretched out a paw to touch his friend's shoulder. "But you're right," he murmured reassuringly, even though he couldn't understand why Toklo was getting so worked up over a flat-face they would never see again. "There's no point in talking to her."

Never again . . . he thought wistfully. *She was so good and kind, but we don't walk the same pathways.*

The sun had begun to slide down the sky by the time Kallik returned, dragging a seal behind her. Ujurak nudged Lusa awake, and the friends clustered eagerly around the catch.

"That's . . . er . . . great, Kallik," Ujurak said, trying to hide his dismay. The seal was the smallest he'd ever seen, not even fully grown. There wasn't nearly enough meat to feed all four of them.

"Yeah . . . brilliant catch!" Lusa added, but her voice sounded hollow.

Toklo just let out a growl as he tore off a chunk of meat.

"Don't say thanks or anything," Kallik muttered to him as they all crouched down to share the catch. "I waited *ages* for this!"

Lusa swallowed a mouthful of the seal meat. "We know you did your best—"

"It doesn't sound like it," Kallik interrupted, her voice rising in frustration. "If this isn't good enough for you, why don't you go and find some berries or hares?"

"You know we can't." Toklo rose to his paws, glowering at the white bear. "There's nothing here but seals! And ice! And more seals and more ice!"

He gave the remains of the seal a contemptuous prod with one paw and started to lumber away.

"Wait," Lusa cried, springing to her paws and scampering after him. "Come back! You're wrong!"

Toklo swung around and loomed over the little black bear. "Wrong, am I?" he challenged her. "If you're so clever, then show me these other things."

Lusa stretched out her muzzle toward him, a sudden intensity in her eyes. *"Listen . . ."* she breathed out.

Ujurak and Kallik exchanged a mystified glance. All the bears fell silent. Ujurak hardly dared to breathe. Then, far in the distance, he heard a faint barking.

"There!" Lusa exclaimed triumphantly.

"I suppose you've made your point," Toklo grumbled as he plodded back to his friends, with Lusa bouncing alongside. "But what is it? And can we eat it?"

They all listened again to the faint barking. Ujurak thought he should remember what animal sounded like that, but the memory escaped him. "Is it seals?" he asked Kallik.

The white bear shook her head, looking puzzled. Then suddenly her eyes brightened. "Walruses!" she exclaimed.

"What?" Lusa's eyes stretched wide with alarm. "They're scary!"

Ujurak's belly lurched, remembering the time that he and Kallik had been attacked by a walrus. Even with two of them to fight back, it had taken all their courage and strength to kill the fearsome creature.

"I know," Kallik responded. "We'll have to make sure we don't get too near them. But walruses never go far out onto the Endless Ice. Hearing them means we must be near land."

New energy flooded through Ujurak. With his friends hard on his paws, he scrambled and scampered over the ice

in the direction of the noise. But however hard they ran, the sound didn't seem to grow any nearer.

"It's much farther away than I hoped," Kallik said.

"The air is so still," Lusa panted as she struggled to keep up with her bigger companions. "Sound travels a long way."

Twilight gathered as the sun sank down and the short day came to an end. But the clouds were breaking up, and the full moon soon appeared, floating high in the sky. The ice glimmered silver under its pale light.

"Let's keep going," Toklo growled. "I don't care where, just so long as we get off this stupid ice."

"Ujurak, can you see any signs?" Lusa asked.

Ujurak halted briefly and scanned the sky, but there was no sign that the spirits were present, only a few faint streaks on the horizon.

"We've hardly seen the spirits since we left the oil rig," he said, half to himself. "Have they given up on us because we've taken too long?" He felt as if a stone were in his belly, pulling him down. "Are we too late?"

"Don't think that!" Lusa encouraged him, pushing her snout into his shoulder. "You can still feel your mother urging you on, can't you? And now we've found a whole new place to explore!"

She bounded off again, her short legs pumping determinedly, and Ujurak followed, catching up to Toklo and Kallik. But their days of journeying and lack of food were sapping their strength. They couldn't keep running for long.

Ujurak thought that the barking of the walruses was a

little clearer, but they were still a long way off when he realized that the bears were all too exhausted to carry on. Lusa had started to lag behind, blinking and shaking her head now and then as if she was trying to keep awake. Kallik was limping after treading on a sharp piece of ice, and even Toklo looked strained.

"We have to rest," Ujurak announced, coming to a halt. "The walruses won't go away."

His friends were too weary to argue. They found a sheltered spot at the foot of another ice ridge and curled up to sleep. As Ujurak closed his eyes, the barking of the walruses continued to echo in his ears, but the land still felt a long way off.

The whining of the wind and a raw chill in the depths of his fur woke Ujurak before the sun rose. Snowflakes whirled in front of his nose; the blizzard lashed his pelt and tore at his body with icy claws.

Beside him Toklo was crouching, with Lusa peering over his shoulder into the eddying snow. "Just what we need," Toklo grunted.

"We can't freeze to death now!" Lusa protested. "Not when we're so close to land. The spirits wouldn't be so cruel."

"We should dig into the snow," Kallik said, from Ujurak's other side. "That way we can keep warm."

For a moment Ujurak thought he was too exhausted to make a single scrape. But desperation gave strength to his paws. Together the four of them began to burrow into the snow at the bottom of the ridge, hollowing out a den.

"Stupid blizzard!" Lusa exclaimed as her paws worked vigorously. "If it weren't for that, we could be on our way toward the walruses again."

She dug even deeper, her hindpaws throwing up a bank of snow behind her, while her head disappeared into the bottom of the hollow. Suddenly she stopped, letting out a startled yelp.

"What's the matter?" Ujurak asked anxiously, afraid that his friend had hurt herself.

Lusa's head popped up again. "Stones!" she squeaked. "Earth!"

For a moment Ujurak gaped at her in disbelief; then he crowded around with Toklo and Kallik to see what the small black bear had found.

Lusa was right. Instead of water, or snow, or more ice, at the bottom of the hole was a layer of gritty pebbles. Ujurak reached down and touched the rough surface, feeling it solid beneath his paw. Thankfulness flooded through him.

We've made it!

As the four bears stood together, too overwhelmed to speak, the bellowing of walruses broke through the sounds of the storm.

"I name this Walrus Rock," Lusa announced solemnly. Scrambling into the hole, she pushed forward her snout to snuff up the smell of the land. Ujurak and Toklo squeezed in beside her; Ujurak closed his eyes and drew the warm scent of stones and earth deep into himself.

"Well," Kallik's voice came cheerfully from the rim of the hollow, "maybe now you'll all stop complaining about eating seals."

Ujurak looked up again, seeing the white bear as a dim shape amid the whirling snow. As he clambered out of the hollow, he could see nothing in all directions except for the same snow-covered landscape they had journeyed over for what seemed like endless days.

Where are all the plants and animals? he asked himself. *How much farther do we have to go?*

Together they enlarged the hollow and huddled inside it while the storm screamed overhead. Two sunrises came and went while the wind whipped over the icy plain, driving the snow along with it.

Ujurak felt the pangs of hunger griping deeper in his belly with every day that passed, and he knew that his companions were suffering, too.

"It wouldn't be so bad if we couldn't hear the walruses," Toklo grumbled as the wind carried another gust of bellowing cries toward them. "I can smell them, too. I can't think of anything except for sinking my teeth into one of them."

Ujurak muttered agreement; he was hungry enough to risk attacking one of the savage creatures for the chance of gorging on the meat.

Kallik groaned and buried her snout deeper into Lusa's fur. All they could do was endure, and hope to sleep away the time until they could carry on.

At last Ujurak woke to silence. Raising his head, he

realized that the wind had dropped. The sun was shining; light reflected from the undisturbed covering of snow that blanketed the ice in every direction.

"Wake up!" Ujurak prodded Toklo, then Kallik and Lusa. "The storm is over."

He hauled himself out of the hollow as his companions woke up, blinking in the bright light and unfolding stiff limbs to follow Ujurak.

Lusa scooped up snow in her paws and rubbed it over her face to wake herself up. "Come on!" she called, bounding enthusiastically away from the den. "It's this way! Let's—" She broke off suddenly as the snowy surface gave way and her small black shape vanished into a drift.

"Oh, for the spirits' sake . . ." Toklo muttered.

He plodded over to where Lusa had disappeared, wading through the fresh, powdery snow. Ujurak watched, half amused and half anxious, as the grizzly plunged his snout into the drift and reared back with Lusa's tail gripped between his jaws.

"Hey, that hurts!" Lusa protested, paws flailing as she emerged with snow clotted all over her black pelt.

Toklo hauled her to the edge of the drift and let go. "Watch where you're putting your paws."

"And don't go running off," Ujurak added as Lusa shook snow from her pelt, scattering it around her in a wide circle. "We're not sure exactly where we are."

"How are we going to find out?" Kallik asked.

Ujurak concentrated, but he couldn't hear or smell the

walruses any more. *Just when it would be useful . . .* And the spirits were still not sending him any signs.

There's one way, he thought, but fear stabbed his heart, colder and harder than sharp splinters of ice. *But I might lose myself forever.*

As the silence dragged out, his fear was thrust aside by guilt. *I can't let my friends down,* he decided. *Not when there's something I can do to help.*

"I'll turn into a bird and fly," he said reluctantly.

"But you don't like changing anymore," Lusa objected.

"That's not the point," Ujurak replied. "It's something I can do, and maybe that makes it my duty." *And if I don't stay in that shape for long, I should be able to remember who I really am.*

Lusa padded over to him and touched her snout to his. "Thanks, Ujurak."

Warmed by the way that his friend understood his hesitation, Ujurak spotted the tiny shape of a seabird in the distance and focused on it. Moments later he felt himself shrinking, and he saw his brown fur vanish to be replaced by the sleek black feathers of a cormorant. His forelegs fanned out into wings, and his hind legs grew bare and skinny. Before his hooked feet could sink into the snow, he took to the air with a mighty flap and soared upward. He let out a harsh cry of triumph as the land fell away beneath him. In spite of his fear he felt the exhilaration of powerful wings bearing him up and the cold air streaming through his feathers.

But I'm a bear. I'm a bear, I'm a bear. I must never forget what I really am.

His friends shrank to three tiny shapes at the foot of Walrus Rock. Higher still, and Ujurak could see that they were on an island, surrounded by the frozen sea. He couldn't tell exactly where the land ended and the ocean began, but he spotted exposed cliffs, and places where it looked as if the snow had been blown to a thin layer. There were no trees, but a few scrawny bushes clung to the cliff face.

Ujurak circled the whole island; at the far side he spotted the walruses, a whole mass of them on a plain near the sea, packed tighter together than grubs under a rock. Swooping down, Ujurak let his gaze travel over their glistening brown bodies, their whiskered faces and curving fangs. He went so low that some of them jerked back their heads and snapped at him.

Oh, no, Ujurak thought, gaining height again with a single flap of his wings. *You're not going to eat cormorant today!*

The walruses' smell gusted over him; he looked down in disgust as they slithered fatly over each other like huge slugs. The babies never stopped squawking, and the bellowing of the full-grown males filled the air like thunder.

Yuck! I'll make sure I never turn into a walrus!

As Ujurak flew back over the cliffs, another cormorant dove at him, her wings folded back as she let out a loud alarm call.

"All right! All right, I'm going!" Ujurak called back, guessing that she had a nest somewhere close by.

Swiftly he flew back inland, pushing down panic for a moment as he wasn't sure of the way back to Walrus Rock.

Then he spotted the familiar twisted shape, with his three friends waiting patiently beside it.

The sun was setting as Ujurak landed in the lee of the rock and let himself change back into bear shape. At first he felt heavy and clumsy, and he missed the soaring freedom of flight, until the comfort of his brown bear shape flowed over him: This was the body he belonged in.

The other bears clustered around him excitedly.

"What did you see?" Lusa demanded.

Ujurak noticed that snow was sifted in her black pelt again. "What have you been doing, rolling in it?" he asked.

Lusa looked shamefaced, not meeting his gaze. "I fell into another drift," she admitted.

"Never mind that." Kallik pushed forward eagerly. "Tell us what you saw."

Ujurak described the island and the cliffs, and the stinking pack of walruses. "Far too many for us to think of hunting," he said.

Toklo looked disappointed, but he didn't argue. "What do you think we should do, then?"

"Make for the center of the island, the highest part," Ujurak replied, jerking his head in that direction. "We might find some bushes there and be able to scrape down to the ground. But it's getting dark. Maybe we should stay here tonight and set off in the morning."

"I'm sick of that den," Toklo growled. "Let's get going now."

"Yes!" Lusa added with an excited little bounce. "We'll be

okay traveling by night."

Ujurak glanced at Kallik, then nodded. Toklo charged off in the lead as they set out for the middle of the island. Privately Ujurak felt that his friends were more confident about journeying in darkness because there was ground beneath the snow now, not ice or water.

"They feel they've come home," Kallik remarked as she fell in beside him.

But they haven't. Ujurak couldn't shake off his misgivings. *None of us have. Maybe we don't even know where home is anymore.*

ENTER THE WORLD OF WARRIORS

Warriors

Sinister perils threaten the four warrior Clans. Into the midst of this turmoil comes Rusty, an ordinary housecat, who may just be the bravest of them all.

Warriors: The New Prophecy

Follow the next generation of heroic cats as they set off on a quest to save the Clans from destruction.

Also available unabridged from Harper Children's Audio

HARPER
An Imprint of HarperCollinsPublishers

Visit www.warriorcats.com for games, Clan lore, and much more!

Manga
Action

SEEKERS
KALLIK'S
ADVENTURE

Polar bear cub Kallik and her brother,
Taqqiq, live in a cozy den nestled
into the side of a snowy hill. Their
mother, Nisa, tells them stories of
the great world beyond their little
den: stories of other bears, endless
snow, and flecks of ice in the sky called
stars. Kallik and Taqqiq can't wait to explore everything,
though Nisa says they're still to venture out. But
when the two cubs sneak they discover some
startling new thing the wild and make a new
—whose life may be in danger!

Discover Seekers online.
Visit www.seekerbears.com
for bear lore, contests,
maps, and more!

www.harpercollinschildrens.com
BOOK NEWS, GAMES, CONTESTS, AND MORE

US $6.99 / $9.25 CAN
ISBN 978-0-06-172383-4

50699

9 780061 723834

TOKYOPOP

HARPER COLLINS

ACTION

Y
YOUTH
AGE 10+